STAN LEE'S KIDS UNIVERSE PRESENTS...

MONSTERS
VS.
KITTENS

DANI JONES

WRITTEN BY: DANI JONES
ARTWORK BY: DANI JONES
COVER BY: DANI JONES

WITHDRAWN

STAN LEE - CREATIVE DIRECTOR
PARIS KASIDOKOSTAS LATSIS- PUBLISHER
GILL CHAMPION - EXECUTIVE PRODUCER
TERRY DOUGAS- PUBLISHER & EDITOR IN CHIEF
EVANGELOS MARINAKIS
MILTIADIS MARINAKIS
ELENI MARINAKIS
EIRINI MARINAKIS
IRINA TAKA
BILLY PICHÉ- VP OF DEVELOPMENT & PRODUCTION
1821 COMICS - EXECUTIVE PRODUCER
POW! ENTERTAINMENT- EXECUTIVE PRODUCER

Monsters vs Kittens. June 2012, published by Stan Lee's Kids Universe. 205 S Beverly Dr #205 Beverly Hills, CA 90212. Copyright 2012 Stan Lee's Kids Universe. All Rights Reserved. All characters, the distinctive likeness thereof and all related indicia are trademarks of Stan Lee's Kids Universe. ISBN: 978-0-9851694-3-5. Printed in China. CPSIA Section 103(a)compliant. www.beaconstar.com/consumer. ID: K0117893. Tracking No.: L2212477-8565

TO MY FAMILY,
AND TO MY MONSTERS/KITTENS -
SALLY, PATRICK, AND GEORGE.

THIS IS A MONSTER.

THIS IS A KITTEN.

MONSTERS ARE BIG.

6

KITTENS ARE SMALL.

KITTENS ARE CLEAN.

MONSTERS ARE MESSY.

MONSTERS SMELL WEIRD.

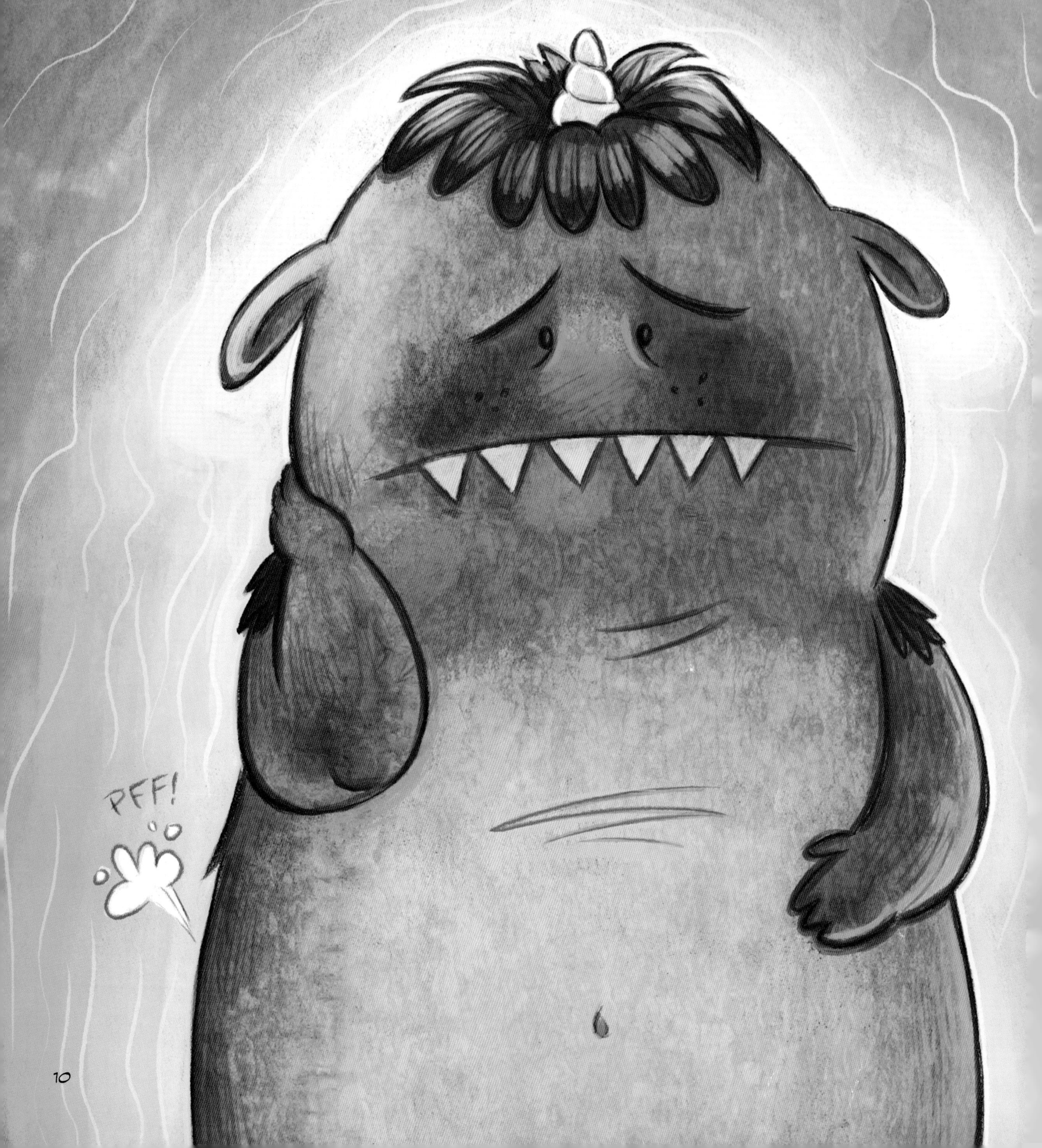

KITTENS DON'T.

(USUALLY)

KITTENS LIKE TO EAT TUNA FISH.
MONSTERS LIKE TO EAT . . .

. . . CHEESEBURGERS.

KITTENS LIKE MICE.

MONSTERS DO NOT.

MONSTERS LIKE TO SWIM.

KITTENS DO NOT.

YOU WOULD THINK THAT
MONSTERS AND KITTENS
HAVE NOTHING IN COMMON
WHATSOEVER, BUT . . .

THEY ARE BOTH WARM AND CUDDLY.

AND THEY LOVE TO CLIMB TREES.

23

KITTENS LIKE TO LIE IN THE SUN,
AND SO DO MONSTERS.

THEY NAP ALL DAY.

AND PLAY ALL NIGHT.

AND THEY DON'T CARE WHAT THEIR FRIENDS LOOK LIKE.

KITTENS LIKE MONSTERS,
AND MONSTERS LIKE KITTENS.